ENTERTA & EDUCA BABIES & TODDLERS

Robyn Gee and Susan Meredith

Designed by Kim Blundell

Illustrated by Sue Stitt, Kim Blundell
and Jan Nesbitt

Cover designed and illustrated by Amanda Barlow

Special consultants: Dr. Peter Hope, Consultant Paediatrician,
John Radcliffe Hospital, Oxford and Hank Williams,
Play Development Consultant.

Contents

In the first part of this book you will find plenty of ideas to help you entertain babies, from birth through toddlerhood and up to the age of 2½. (The second part of the book contains similar but more advanced ideas suitable for the 2½-5 age group.) None of the activities requires a great deal of preparation or special equipment. The time you have for playing will be limited and, in any case, children in this age group appreciate variety of entertainment most of all.

It is now known that babies and toddlers are capable of much more than was thought hitherto and that in fact children learn more and at greater speed during their pre-school years than at any other time in their lives. Even the very youngest babies are ready to start learning about the world around them and can become bored unless someone provides them with the stimulation that they cannot seek out for themselves. The first few pages of the book in particular concentrate on ways of entertaining babies in the first few months of life.

It is not always immediately obvious how certain activities can help a baby to learn. The introduction to each of the topics in the book includes a brief outline of the activities' learning value. Quite often their greatest value lies in the emotional satisfaction babies get from having a parent's full attention and interest, even for only short periods.

No very precise guidelines have been given on the suitable age for each activity, as babies develop at widely differing rates. However, they do tend to go through certain stages of development in roughly the same order so that while it is hard to say exactly when a stage will be reached, it is easier to predict which stage will be reached next. The chart at the back of this section lists some of the stages of development.

Adults can play a very important role in helping a baby or toddler to practise new skills and to learn to play constructively by giving help and encouragement, and by providing the necessary materials. It is worth bearing in mind, however, that even babies need freedom to explore their environment in their own way and that they will develop basic skills without your having to provide constant stimulation. Whatever you do, you cannot make babies reach a certain stage of development sooner than their bodies and brains will allow.

It is important that parents recognize their own needs as well as their child's and do not feel obliged to provide activities that they would not enjoy themselves. Babies and toddlers are very sensitive to mood and can be confused and hurt by a contradiction between a parent's actions and attitude. For a joint activity to be successful, it has to be enjoyable for both of you.

THINGS TO LOOK AT

Having things to look at provides very young babies with one of their chief sources of stimulation, especially when they are still too young to be able to hold things.

People used to think that newborn babies could not see at all but it is now known that they are simply long-sighted and can only see clearly things that are about 25cm (10in) from their nose. They respond to very bright colors, though everything looks rather two-dimensional to them at first. By the time they are six months old, their eyesight is almost as good as adults'.

Giving babies plenty of things to look at not only helps to keep them entertained but also helps them begin to learn to recognize objects and people, and improves their eyesight by exercising and strengthening the muscles used for focusing.

Faces

The distance babies can see at birth happens to be the approximate distance from the crook of a person's arm to their face. Research has shown that babies are more interested in looking at the human face than any other object.

By looking at a baby as you hold him, and smiling and talking, you give him practice in focusing, help him to get to know the human face and you encourage him to return the smiles and so take one of the first steps in communicating with people.

First toys

Apart from faces, young babies have a definite preference for certain other types of objects to look at. These do not need to be real toys as everything is new to them and potentially interesting.

Always give the baby plenty of time to respond to the things you show him. Babies have much slower reactions than adults. You can try tucking objects down the side of his crib or buggy mattress.* Don't worry, this will not make him squint.

Babies like things that:

— have bold, clear features. Draw a face on a paper plate or use a photograph of a face.

— are brightly colored.

— are shiny, for example, aluminum foil or stainless steel.

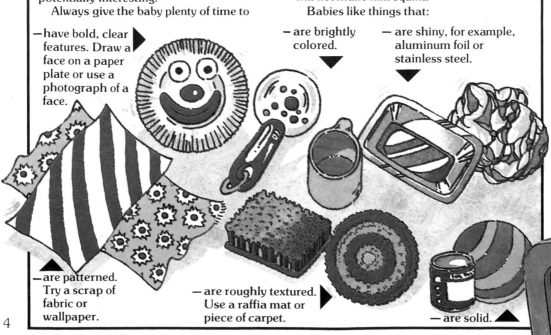

— are patterned. Try a scrap of fabric or wallpaper.

— are roughly textured. Use a raffia mat or piece of carpet.

— are solid.

4

Babies start swatting things at about three months old so beware of anything that could be harmful if it were grabbed or fell down. See page 12 for more about safety.

Mobiles

Once a baby's head stops flopping over to one side when she is lying on her back, you can start hanging objects above her crib, buggy or changing table or you can hang them near her chair. It is useful to have ideas for making your own mobiles so you can provide variety.

For a very simple mobile, just hang a single, lightweight object, such as a balloon, on a piece of thread from a drawing pin in the ceiling. The lighter the mobile, the more it will move in a breeze, catching the baby's attention.

For a more elaborate mobile, try fixing a hook in the ceiling, hanging a coat-hanger from it on a piece of string and tying a number of objects to the hanger with thread. It may take you a while to get the objects to balance. Try to arrange them so as to emphasize the difference in their size, shape, color and texture, and replace or rearrange them regularly to prevent boredom. Here are a few ideas for things to use:

Cardboard or fabric cut or folded into interesting shapes and decorated with felt pen, gummed shapes, glitter or sequins.

Aluminum foil, slightly crumpled up and/or with holes made in it.

Christmas decorations
Balloons
Foil bottle tops
Yoghurt cartons
Ribbons

Cover coat-hanger with colored paper and tinsel.

Foil bottle tops on thread with knot in end.

Crib-hangers

A good way of giving a young baby things to look at in her crib is to attach them to a length of string or elastic stretched tightly across the crib and fastened securely to the bars at either side. You can thread bulldog clips on to the string and clip the objects up or tie them on. If you use elastic for this, they will bounce if they are touched.

You can use almost any lightweight object, including the ones suggested above for mobiles.* Again, emphasize the contrast between the objects and change them often.

Spiral cut from circle of cardboard.

Large buttons on strong thread with large knot at end. Remove when baby starts grasping.

Rubber glove stuffed with tissue paper.

Knot thread through base of yoghurt carton.

Strainer

Measuring spoons

Providing variety

This is essential for young babies because their attention span is extremely short. Besides having a variety of things to look at, they need to spend time in different places and positions.

Spells in a crib or buggy can be alternated with periods on a mat or soft rug on the floor, in a baby chair or, from about six weeks old, propped up securely by cushions or pillows in a buggy, the corner of an armchair or the middle of a bed.* Try to position the baby so she can look at a room from various angles and take her from room to room with you so she can watch what you are doing. Many babies are happier if there are other people around and activity going on. Many like being carried upright so they can see things from high up, over your shoulder. Lamps, mirrors and the television are often favorite objects to look at.

Peekaboo

Babies love the surprise of seeing someone's face suddenly appear from behind their hands and the accompanying "boo". They begin to learn from this that things continue to exist even when they cannot see them. The game is an excellent way of communicating with a young baby. Vary it by peeping out from behind the furniture. As he gets older, the baby will start to take the initiative at "peekaboo".

Pop-up toys

These provide some of the same pleasures and functions as "peekaboo". Try drawing a face on a wooden spoon and popping it up and down inside an empty paper towel roll. You could stick on some yarn or cotton balls and brighten up the roll by sticking colored paper or fabric round it.

Things that move

Babies are fascinated by things that move and may attempt to track something dangling in their field of vision almost from birth. Try dangling a brightly colored object about 25cm (10in) from the baby's face, at first moving it slowly from side to side, later in other directions.

Older babies enjoy watching the movement of bubbles, balloons and balls, especially if you use these to topple blocks or bowling pins.

Going out

Taking a baby out in a buggy gives her a whole new range of stimulating things to look at. Even at a very early age she will probably enjoy looking at the goods hanging up in the shops and at the people you meet.

If you put her in the garden in her buggy, try to position it so she can watch the movement of leaves, washing, shadows or clouds.

THINGS TO LISTEN TO

Babies can hear quite well right from birth, although they may not appear to, and their attention span for listening is even shorter than for looking. They can hear high-pitched sounds better than low-pitched ones at first.

One of the best uses of sound for young babies is to soothe and relax. Gentle talking and music are good for this, and you can buy "soothing sounds" tapes.

Providing sounds for babies to listen to helps them learn to tell where sounds are coming from, which they cannot do at first. As early as four weeks, some babies start turning towards sounds they hear.

Voices

Babies' favorite sound is the human voice. It is thought that, by the age of six weeks, they can probably recognize their mother by her voice alone and that their first smiles are produced as much in response to a voice as a face.

Besides calming and reassuring them, talking to babies right from birth lays the foundation for their own ability to talk later. They enjoy "baby talk" because they like rhythm, rhyme and repetition, but don't worry if you find that difficult to do, as they also need to hear proper speech. A young baby may be happy to listen to you talking to someone else for a while, eg on the telephone. It is also worth singing songs, reciting nursery rhymes and playing records or cassettes of these from birth. For more about talking to babies, see pages 14-17.

Rattles and other sounds

Besides choosing from the many sound-producing toys you can buy, it is easy to improvise your own to provide variety. Until a baby can hold things, you obviously have to make them sound for her.

Try putting any of the following into empty containers and sealing the tops firmly.**

Rice
Pasta
Beans
Lentils
Salt
Water
Earth
Sand
Pebbles
Flower seeds
Clothes pins
Bottle tops
Paper clips
Buttons
Beads
Marbles

You could also buy a little bell from a pet shop, sew it to ribbon or elastic and add it to a mobile or crib-hanger, or even fasten it round the baby's wrist for short periods. Once the baby starts grasping, move it out of reach. She could choke on it.

Make a point of letting the baby listen to any of the ordinary household objects you are using, for example, keys being jangled, paper crumpled or drinks stirred.

Loud noises

Babies tend to be frightened by sudden loud noises, such as a doorbell ringing, or even a cough or a laugh. Very high or low-pitched noises can also scare them.

On the other hand, more continuous loud noises made, for example, by a washing machine, vacuum cleaner or running tap may fascinate and quieten a fretful baby.

Telling where sounds come from

You can give a baby useful practice in locating sounds by speaking or making a noise at different points in the room, starting close to him. Always show him afterwards what made each sound so he comes to associate it with its source.

Don't carry on doing this for too long or make it seem like a test and don't worry, either, if the baby does not appear to respond for several months.

7

THINGS TO FEEL AND HOLD

Babies start learning about the world through their sense of touch right from birth, although they cannot hold things until they are about three months old. Picking up different objects, handling them and putting them down again is a complex skill that babies spend much of their first year trying to master, as their muscles strengthen and their eyesight and co-ordination between their eyes and hands improve. The way newborn babies try to grasp objects put into the palm of their hand is not deliberate, but is an involuntary reflex action.

Sock stuffed with tissue paper.

The best thing you can do to ensure that a baby's manipulative skills develop to the full is simply to provide as wide a variety of different, safe objects as possible for practising on. Babies may not appear to do very much with the objects but they are learning all the time not only what they feel like but how they behave when treated in a certain way. This is necessary before they can begin to use objects successfully as tools.

Swatting

Before they can hold things, babies enjoy swatting. Try attaching some foil and a sock stuffed with tissue paper or elastic and adding them to the baby's crib-hanger (see page 5) so that they are within arm's reach. At first he will hit the objects by chance but, as he notices them moving, he will gradually realize that there is a connection between what he is seeing and what his hands are doing, and he will start to reach out deliberately.

People

Above all else, most babies like the sensation of being held and cuddled. It is thought that the grasp reflex babies are born with may date from prehistoric times, when they clung to their mothers' fur for safety. In many parts of the world it is still the norm for mothers to carry their babies constantly. The most practical way of doing this is to use a sling. Even the most fretful babies are often soothed and comforted by the closeness, warmth, movement and possibly heartbeat, which they have been used to in the womb.

Massage

Massage can give babies a feeling of physical and emotional well-being, just as it does older people. It is advisable to learn the technique at a baby massage class, though there are books on the subject. The relaxing effect of massage probably benefits fretful babies most. It is best to massage the baby without his clothes in a very warm room though you can massage through clothes if necessary. You may be able to massage some parts of the body with the baby in your lap or arms.

Things to lie on

As very young babies spend so much time in a crib or buggy. It is worth providing them with extra-comfortable bed-clothes, the softer and warmer to the touch, the better. Some people recommend sheepskins. For kicking sessions on the floor, a young baby needs a soft rug or blanket to lie on. As she gets older, let her feel different surfaces such as carpet or grass.

Weather permitting, it is good for babies to spend time with no clothes on so they can get to know the different parts of their body and feel the air against their skin.

Whiffle balls

Foil dish with face cut out.

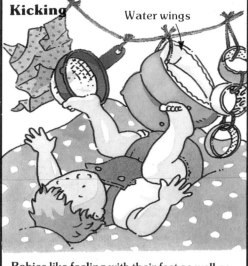

Kicking

Water wings

If the objects make a noise when he hits them, so much the better. Use rattles, too, or buy bells from a pet shop and add them to the balloon. You can also press tiny bells through the largest hole in a whiffle ball (make sure they cannot come out again) and then suspend several of these.

Swatting is important for developing hand/eye co-ordination and also because it makes babies feel less passive as they realize their actions can affect the things around them.

Babies like feeling with their feet as well as their hands and enjoy kicking against things that move. These need to be quite large as the baby cannot see them. Try suspending crumpled paper and inflatable water wings or cushions across the bottom of the crib on strong elastic, and attach bells or rattles to them.

Kicking in a bouncing chair is enjoyable both for the movement itself and for the sense of control it gives a baby when she realizes it is her kicking that causes the movement.

Feel-cloths and comforters

Having different sorts of fabric to feel can provide a baby with a variety of interesting sensations. Try silk, satin, velvet, fur and stretchy materials. He may enjoy having your clothes to hold because they smell of you.

You might like to sew some scraps of different fabric together to make a "feel-cloth". It is often a piece of fabric that a baby adopts as his special "comforter" because of its texture and smell. This is quite normal. Experts refer to comforters as "transitional objects" because they help a baby make the psychological transition from total dependence on the people who look after him to independence.

First attempts at holding

As soon as a baby starts holding his hands open instead of fisted, you can start putting small, light objects into them. He may be able to hold the objects for a few seconds although he will probably not look at what his hands are doing. This is the stage at which rattles are most useful. The sound of the rattle as he waves his arms around prompts him to look at his hands and make the connection between hands, eyes and ears. Give the baby practice at holding in each hand. He will not show a preference for one hand until well past his first birthday.

9

Taking hold of things

Babies usually start trying to take hold of things at about four months. Watch out for this and put objects alongside the baby in her crib or buggy. Until she can grasp them successfully, you could perhaps tie them to the crib bars so they cannot move away when she touches them. At this stage swinging objects across the crib will only frustrate her and a crib gym like the one shown above can be a good buy.

When you hold something out for the baby to take, you need to be patient. You may notice her glancing backwards and forwards between the object and her hand. This is because she has to measure the distance between the two. Give her the chance at least to touch the object before you help by handing it to her.

The best position for a baby to practise picking things up is sitting in a baby chair, preferably one with a tray on which you can put a selection of toys. Don't give her more than two or three to begin with or she will feel confused and, in any case, she needs practice in holding and handling as well as picking up. Replace the objects one by one to stave off boredom.

Once a baby can hold things, safety becomes especially important as she will put everything in her mouth.* Her mouth is more sensitive than her fingers at this stage so she can learn more about the objects by doing this.

Ideas for things to hold

Some babies are not content to hold and examine one object for more than a few seconds at a time and drop things constantly through boredom as well as incompetence. Variety is all-important and you need to have a large supply of safe, household objects always on hand. It is worth keeping a collection of things the baby can play with ready in each room. Below and opposite are some ideas.

Living room
Books. Babies are fascinated by hinges and love opening and shutting books, and turning the pages, besides looking at them.
Old magazines and catalogues
Cotton spools. Try threading them on string or ribbon.
Ribbon*
Elastic

Ball of yarn. Make sure the end cannot work loose.*
Blank cassettes
Playing cards
Coasters
Cushions*

Bathroom
Baby's personal possessions: sponge, toothbrush, comb, hairbrush, diapers.
Soap dish. With soap inside, this makes a rattle.
Talcum powder cans*

Cream jars*
Plastic bottles*
Toilet paper tube
Clean towel
Nail brush
Drop-eye bath
Strip of bandage
Roll of adhesive tape

*See page 12 for notes on safety and hygiene.

Select objects for the differences in their shape, size, weight and texture (rough, smooth, soft, hard, stiff, stretchy, for example). Bear in mind, too, what makes things interesting to look at (see pages 4 and 6) and to listen to (see page 7) so the baby learns to use his different senses together.

Try to develop an eye for anything that is a potential new "toy" such as packaging, an empty container or the lining from a chocolate box. Hide away familiar playthings when they become boring and they may seem fresh and exciting again a few days later.

If you have a number of small objects that would be unsafe to give to the baby individually or that he keeps dropping, you could try threading them on to a shoe-lace or length of string and tying the ends firmly. Or you could tie the objects to curtain rings and sew these securely to a strong piece of plain fabric or a plain cushion.

Kitchen*

Spoons (plastic, metal and wooden)	Foil dishes
Yoghurt cartons and margarine tubs	Egg cartons
	Tea caddy
Unopened packages, cans or strong bags of food	Coffee can
	Biscuit pan
	Fish slice
Stainless steel egg cups	Potato masher
	Ladle
Washed fruit and vegetables	Spatulas
	Sieve
Rubber rings from preserving jars	Colander
	Strainer
Plastic containers	Whisk
Plastic or paper cups and plates	Funnel
	Pastry brush
Metal teapot	Paper cake cases
Metal kettle	Doilies
Saucepans and lids	Drinking straws
Egg poaching pan	Paper towel roll
Cupcake or muffin pans	Rubber gloves
	New dish-cloth
Trays	Clean tea towel
Ice-cube tray	Napkin rings
	Place mats

Miscellaneous

Plastic bottles. To make a bubble bottle, fill a transparent, screw-topped bottle with water and a squirt of dish washing liquid, or, for a different sort of bubble, use a tablespoon of cooking oil. You could add food coloring too.

Rattles, home-made as well as bought. See page 7 for ideas.

Clean, empty boxes, jars, cans and bottles (not glass) with or without lids. Hinged lids are the most fun.

Balls of different sizes (ping-pong, tennis, football)

Paper of all sorts, except newspaper, for crumpling, tearing, rustling, hiding behind.

Packages. Wrap a favorite toy loosely in one or two thicknesses of paper without taping it down. Or put it in a paper bag.

Ball of string. Make sure the end cannot work loose.*

Mirrors. Only let him have unbreakable baby mirrors to hold.

Windows and walls. Hold the baby up so he can hit, stroke, wipe and scratch.

Balloons, not fully blown up.

Pieces of well sanded wood.

Rulers (wooden, plastic and metal)

Roll of adhesive tape

Wicker baskets and bowls

New flowerpots and saucers

New dustpan and brush

Scraps of fabric

Clothes pins

Large pebbles

Bunch of keys

11

Getting more skilled

As the baby's manipulative skills improve, you can help in a variety of ways.

★ Offer him objects at different angles so he has to work out how best to take them.

★ Give him larger or heavier things that he has to get both hands to.

★ Give him things with holes to poke his fingers into (whiffle ball, draining spoon) or put his hands and feet through (bangle, roll of adhesive tape, wrist band).

★ Hand him a second object and he will gradually learn not to drop the first but to hold an object in each hand and, eventually, to hold two things in one hand.

Food

Meal times are a good opportunity to practise manipulative skills. Finger feeding and holding a cup are two of the first things a baby can do for herself. She can also practise holding a spoon well before she can feed herself efficiently with it.

Making a mess with food can be seen as the very earliest form of creative play. It is also thought that being allowed to do this helps to avoid faddy eating habits.

The pincer grip

By about nine months, most babies are developing the ability to hold things between finger and thumb, pincer-like, rather than in their palm only. To master the pincer grip they need practice with very small, fine objects. For safety's sake, things to eat are the best. Try small pieces of potato and carrot, peas, bread, crackers and dry cereal. The baby will also be fascinated by lengths of wool, thread or string.*

Safety and hygiene

Once a baby starts reaching out for things, it is vitally important to be aware of the possible dangers of any object he might get hold of. If you are in doubt about something, don't leave it lying around.

★ Babies put everything in their mouths. Never let a baby have anything small enough to swallow or choke on, or put in his nose or ears. This includes larger objects from which small parts could get detached when tugged or chewed. The safest containers are ones with screw tops. Babies cannot usually unscrew these until they are about 18 months old but they can lift press-on tops earlier.

Don't give a baby objects painted with paint that may contain lead, avoid newsprint and wash out empty bottles very thoroughly. Avoid completely bottles that have had bleach or cleaning fluids in them.

★ Don't let him have anything that could suffocate him. This includes plastic bags, and cushions or pillows if there is any chance he might fall on top of them.

★ Beware of anything that could strangle him or get wound round his fingers or toes and cut off the blood supply. Don't leave him playing alone with things like ribbon.

★ Avoid pointed objects that he could dig in his skin, put down his throat or poke in his eyes, ears or nose, and objects with sharp edges that he could cut himself on. Throw away yoghurt cartons when they crack.

★ Avoid objects heavy enough to hurt if he dropped them on himself.

★ Make sure all his playthings are clean. Objects that have been in contact with food are the main danger and it is safest to sterilize cooking utensils before giving them to a baby under nine months. Just wash other things regularly in dish washing liquid or baking soda, rinse and drip dry.

*See "safety" above.

Learning to let go

Playing ball

Most babies cannot let go of things deliberately until they are about ten months old. The best way to help a baby do this is to put your open hand beneath something she is holding so she can feel it resting on a flat surface.

Once she has got the idea, you can start playing games of "give and take". Encourage her to let go by asking her to give you what she is holding and by doing something amusing with it before you give it back again.

Once a baby can let go of things, she may be ready for an elementary game of ball. To begin with, sit her on the floor with her legs apart and gently throw a ball so that it lands between them. She will probably try to pat it, if not throw it back to you.

You can also throw the ball gently into her lap as she sits in her chair. She will be delighted to have "caught" it and will push it off again for you to retrieve.

Dropping things

This becomes a favorite pastime when a baby realizes she can let go. Babies do not drop things to annoy but because they are practising a new skill, are curious to discover what happens to the things they drop and enjoy the social, taking-turns aspect of the game as you hand things back to them.

When you get fed up with picking things up, you could attach a favorite toy to one end of a length of string, tie the other end to the high chair or buggy and try showing the baby how to haul it up again when she has dropped it.*

Alternatively, provide a number of things all at once for her to drop. Include light objects such as paper or balloons as well as heavier ones, things that roll (plastic bottles), bounce (balls) and stay still (cushions, bean bags). To encourage her to aim, try giving her a largish container to drop the things into. A metal tray in the bottom of the container makes an interesting sound.

Emptying and filling

This usually becomes a major preoccupation around a baby's first birthday. Provide containers of different sizes and plenty of suitable-sized objects to empty out of them and put back in again, such as blocks, carrots, clothes-pins, socks, disposable diapers or playing cards.

The baby will also enjoy unpacking shopping and emptying cupboards. It is worth re-organizing at least one cupboard of household things, perhaps in the kitchen, so he can be allowed to empty it while you work. He may also be intrigued by draw-string bags that he can just get his hand inside.

LEARNING TO TALK

Learning to talk is one of the key developments of a child's first three years and is vital to normal social, emotional and intellectual development.

The rate at which individual children learn to talk varies widely, as does that of all other aspects of development. It depends on temperament and the physical development of the parts of the body used for speech as well as on intellectual ability and stimulation from the environment. It is worth remembering that early progress has no particular bearing on later ability.

Babies start learning language long before they can say any words. Newborn babies prefer the sound of the human voice to any other and talking to them right from birth can play a valuable part in their language development. It not only helps them to learn the rhythms, patterns and intonations of speech but also conveys the idea that talking is a pleasant social activity, which makes them want to participate. To reinforce this idea, it is important to spend some time talking directly to the baby and looking at her while you talk so she feels she has your individual attention. This will also help her to learn the facial expressions that accompany speech.

The suggestions on the following pages may give you some useful starting points for talking to a baby, especially if you feel awkward about talking to someone who cannot reply with words. Babies do respond with a great variety of sounds, however, and listening carefully to these may encourage you to talk back. The charts on pages 42-47 will give you an idea of some of the stages in babies' speech development.

Don't force yourself to oversimplify what you are saying or to use baby talk if this does not come naturally to you. Don't worry either about constantly repeating yourself. Repetition plays an important part in language learning and babies seem to enjoy it.

Things to talk about

When you are doing something for the baby, such as dressing or bathing him, try talking to him about what you are doing. Ask him questions even though you have to supply the answers for him. Show him things and describe them to him, explaining what they are for. When he is old enough to sit in a chair and watch you, you can even give him running commentaries on what you are doing.

Let's just take your diaper off.

First conversations

Babies need to absorb the patterns of talk as well as individual sounds. If they hear plenty of talking, they soon learn that people speak in turn, with pauses in between. Once a baby has started making deliberate sounds, you can give him practice in making "conversation" by saying something, pausing and waiting for him to respond. When he responds, you reply.

Now, is it time for your supper?

Toys

Certain toys are especially useful for encouraging talking. From about six months, most babies enjoy looking in mirrors. These encourage them to be aware of their mouths and so make sounds.

An unbreakable mirror in a colored plastic frame is a good buy.

Rhymes and songs

Learning the rhythms of speech is an important part of learning to talk and nursery rhymes often mimic and emphasize these rhythms. Repetition of the same words over and over again helps babies to recognize particular sounds and eventually to realize that certain sounds have certain meanings. Rhymes and songs with actions to go with them give extra clues as to meaning. (See pages 39-41.)

> Pat-a-cake
> Pat-a-cake
> Baker's man . . .

Books

> Look, there's a little boy digging in the sand.

It is worth looking at books even with a very young baby. Talk about the pictures just as you would with an older child. A simple picture always accompanied by the same word or words is a great aid to realizing that words have meaning. Later, books provide opportunities to learn new words. Read simple stories, too. Eventually the child will start joining in. (See pages 18-20 for more about books.)

From about **12 months**, toy telephones are helpful and making soft toys and puppets speak can also encourage conversation.

To make a finger puppet, cut out a semi-circle of cardboard or felt, curl it into a tube shape and stick it so it fits your finger. Draw or stick on the features.

Two telephones linked by plastic tubing allow you to talk from room to room.

Starting to understand

Babies have to understand quite a lot of language before they can say anything themselves. They learn the meaning of a word by hearing it used repeatedly in different sentences but always associated with the same thing. Saying a single word over and over again in an attempt to make a baby understand it or to imitate the sound before she understands its meaning is not very useful.

From about eight months onwards, when a baby is starting to understand a few sounds and words, it is worth taking a bit of trouble to help her understanding develop.

★ Stress the key words in your sentences and try not to replace them with pronouns.

> Where's the cup?
> Oh, there's the cup.

★ Use the baby's name instead of "you" or "your".

> Here's a biscuit for Emily.

> Here's a biscuit for Mummy.

★ Exaggerate your intonation and facial expressions, and match your words with actions.

> . . . high up in the air.

> . . . a red block and a blue block.

★ Talk about things the baby is looking at and about things that interest her such as toys or food.

First words

Most babies use their first real words (that is, sounds with specific meanings attached to them) round about their first birthday. First words are often surprisingly difficult to identify, as it is hard to sort out the accidental from the intentional. They are nearly always labels – names for people, animals and things that are important to them, though social words such as "bye-bye", "no" and "thank you" are often among the first as well. You may find that some words have a very general meaning. Many babies start off by using the same word for any type of food or drink.

Some babies learn lots of words as soon as they begin to speak but it is more usual to learn between one and three a month for the first few months. Some words may only be used for a few days or weeks and then disappear from their vocabulary for quite a time. If a baby is concentrating hard on learning to walk, progress with talking may slow down temporarily.

At around 18 months, toddlers often start to learn new words much more rapidly and by the time they are two may know as many as 200 words. During this period they also learn to use more varied intonation to indicate whether a word is a label, a greeting, a demand or a question.

★ The more effort you make to understand the baby's first attempts at words, the harder she will try to say more.

Moo, moo

Do you want a drink?

★ Babies often invent words. Don't correct these or pretend not to understand or the baby will be confused and discouraged. They will be replaced by the proper words eventually.

Banban

★ The pronunciation of words is often simplified. Babies often leave consonants off the beginning or end of words and some children have difficulty with certain consonants until they are about five. Don't try to make a child pronounce words correctly, though you could give the right version in your reply.

'poon

Yes, I see. You've got a spoon.

Look, there's a cat.

★ Help the baby to use the words she knows whenever possible and use them in your own conversation.

Putting words together

Shortly before their second birthday, children often start putting two words together to make their meaning clearer; soon after it they may begin to form simple sentences. From now on their range of vocabulary and ability to combine words, use grammar and take part in dialogue steadily improve, provided they get enough encouragement and stimulation.

Gradually they realize that words can be used to describe actions (verbs), where things are (prepositions), who owns what (possessives) and what things are like (adjectives). You may notice a child introducing a different part of speech or aspect of grammar (such as the past tense or plurals) and practising it intensively before moving on to something else.

★ Make language as interesting as possible by making time to have conversations and taking questions seriously and trying to answer them.

What's this made of?

It's made of metal but it's got plastic wheels.

Games to play

These are good for developing understanding, encouraging first words and extending vocabulary. The conversation involved and the repetition of words in context are particularly helpful.

Asking games. Once a baby understands a few words and starts "asking" for things with sounds or gestures, you can turn asking into a game. Sit opposite the baby on the floor, put a ball or other toy in front of him, then hold out your hands and ask him to pass it to you. If he does, roll it back, then ask him to pass it again. Once he gets the idea, wait for him to "ask" before rolling it back.

Fetching games. With a mobile baby, you can extend asking games to become fetching games. Choose an object the baby can see and that he knows the name for and ask him to fetch it for you. Pointing helps in this game but, up to about twelve months, babies tend to look at the pointing finger rather than what it is pointing at.

Once the baby can fetch things that are visible, you can ask him to fetch things that are out of sight but are always kept in the same place. Later, he will be able to look for things that are not kept anywhere in particular.

Hiding and finding games. Start these very simply, as it takes babies a long time to realize that things are still there even when they cannot see them. At first, let the baby see where you are hiding something and always hide it in the same place, perhaps leaving a bit showing. Once he has got the idea, change the hiding place but still let him see where it is. Eventually this will develop into hide and seek, with you taking it in turns to hide things.

Copying games. Babies and toddlers learn a tremendous amount by copying people. Try sitting in front of a big mirror together. Point to the different parts of your body and encourage the baby to copy you, while you name the parts. Later you can play copying games with actions such as jumping and bending to help develop understanding and use of verbs.

Toddlers often enjoy making happy, sad or cross faces in front of a mirror and this helps them learn to understand that faces can express how people feel.

★ Don't restrict your own vocabulary too much. Toddlers understand much more than they can express and learn words by hearing them in context.

★ Don't make a child correct mistakes of grammar. She will only be put off talking. She will learn good grammar by hearing it spoken around her.

★ Don't interrupt or finish the sentence if a child is struggling for words. The process of talking actually helps children to form new concepts.

You hold the wrench while I use the pliers.

I gived you a letter.

Yes, you gave me a letter.

Tom can't lift it . . . 'cos it's heavy.

BOOKS, PICTURES AND STORIES

It is never too early to start showing a baby books. Look at them together as soon as you can balance both the baby and the book on your knee.

To begin with, small babies get as much enjoyment from the movement of the pages turning, the noise of the paper and the sound of your voice, as you talk or read, as they do from the pictures, which they see as colors, shapes and patterns.

Gradually the shapes become familiar and recognizable and they start to associate specific sounds with each shape. Then they learn to turn the pages by themselves, to point to things they recognize, to name things and eventually to listen to and join in stories.

The best reason for introducing babies to books is that they enjoy them. Many parents find that books are the single most effective way of keeping their baby happily entertained. But babies and toddlers can also learn a great deal from looking at books.

Books help to develop their visual understanding and ability to notice detail. They are also very valuable in the development of language skills, helping them learn to listen, understand and speak and encouraging a desire to communicate. They broaden their horizons by stimulating the imagination, helping them to make sense of situations they have experienced and introducing them to new ones, and by showing them how other people feel and behave.

Later on, books will have a vital role to play in a child's more formal education. Early enjoyment of them will help to form a good groundwork for this.

It is worth remembering, even with this very young age group, that there is no point in trying to force books on a child who would clearly prefer to be doing something else. There is always the risk that you may put him off books.

Choosing books

First picture books. To start with, choose a few books that have clear, simple, colorful illustrations of objects or animals that are part of a baby's everyday world. There should be only one or two illustrations per page and no confusing detail. From as early as three months, the baby will be able to focus briefly on the pictures. Include in this early collection one or two board and bath books which will stand up to handling and chewing.

From about 12 months, as the baby acquires more words, he will gradually be able to cope with more and more complicated pictures.

Catalogues. These are often very popular with babies, who particularly enjoy seeing things like other babies and familiar toys, clothes and furniture. They also enjoy tearing the paper. Colorful magazines and photograph albums can also be good entertainment.

Pop-up books. Pop-ups, books with flaps to lift and tags to pull, "feely" books, squeaky books, cloth, board and bath books are all good for getting babies interested and involved in books. They need to be tough if they are to last long.

Nursery rhyme and action rhyme books. These are invaluable for reminding you of old favorites and perhaps introducing you to new ones. They usually remain popular for a long time so choose a good sturdy edition with detailed illustrations.

Making your own books

This is a good cheap way of providing babies with plenty of variety in their library. Punch holes in pieces of card and thread them together with string, yarn or ribbon to make a simple book.

First story books. Talking about pictures in books will lead on naturally to reading stories. You will probably be able to start introducing some very simple stories from about 15 months onwards. Some toddlers find it impossible to sit still and listen, however, while others will listen to stories they do not even understand, enjoying the sound and rhythm of the words.

Choose stories with few words and plenty of pictures which do a lot of the story-telling work. The words will only gradually become as important as the pictures. Stories which repeat catchy, rhythmical phrases over and over again give toddlers something to listen for and enjoy even when they cannot really follow the story-line. Many traditional folk tales do this.

Try out as wide a variety of different stories as you can to see what the child prefers. Borrowing books from a library allows you to do this at no expense.

Stories involving familiar, everyday routines are usually popular with small children. They like to explore how like or unlike other people they are. They may also enjoy fantasy stories. It is worth watching out for, and taking seriously, any sign of a child being disturbed or frightened by a story.

A small scrap book or photograph album also makes a good baby book. The kind of album that has a single plastic pocket per page is ideal for small babies.

Select pictures of things you know the baby particularly enjoys looking at to put in the book. Include your own photographs and drawings of familiar objects.

You could make a "first words" book for the baby. As soon as he can say a word, stick a picture of it in the book. This will also act as a record for you. Write the word beneath the picture so he can gradually absorb the idea that words are written down as well as spoken.

Information books. It is useful for a child to realize that books are a source of factual information as well as stories. Once he starts to outgrow his first simple picture books, replace them with some information books. Zoos, farms and vehicles are popular subjects. He may also enjoy the pictures in nature books aimed at older children.

Books are also helpful for learning about things like colors, shapes and sizes and, by the age of two-and-a-half, it is worth having alphabet and numbers books too.

Old Christmas, birthday and postcards can also be made into books. Cut the backs off, make holes down one side and thread them together.

Looking at books together

The best way of encouraging a baby to like books is to look at them together, as often as the baby wants to and you can find the time. She will enjoy the physical closeness and the feeling of shared experience, and this can help to strengthen the emotional links between you.

You can gradually introduce special times of day for looking at books together. They can help to quieten a toddler down before a nap or bedtime and also provide a useful means of resting without sleeping. Books can also be a great help in passing the time on journeys or whenever you have to sit and wait for something.

Looking at books alone

It is worth encouraging a baby from the beginning to look at books by herself. This starts with simply playing with board, bath or cloth books but once she can turn the pages she may be happy to spend short periods looking at the pictures by herself. This is more likely to happen if she is used to seeing the people around her looking at books.

It is important that her books are kept where she can reach them easily, perhaps in a decorated box in a cosy reading corner.

Telling stories

It is a good idea to accustom children to listening to stories that are not written in books. These can help to develop the imagination and it is useful to learn the skill of listening and understanding without a visual aid.

Most toddlers love hearing stories about themselves and the people close to them. These help them to develop a sense of identity, to use their memories and to picture the past. Photographs can provide a helpful starting point for telling family stories.

Tapes

Many toddlers enjoy listening to tapes, especially those you have compiled yourself. They are useful for times when you cannot give a child your full attention, such as on car journeys, and for encouraging resting and going to sleep. Keep any stories very short and intersperse them with rhymes and songs.

Television

At first, babies see television pictures as changing colors and patterns but they slowly begin to make sense of the jumble of images and sounds and some time during their second year will probably start to watch some programs with interest.

Television has a lot to contribute to a child's understanding and imaginative development. Stories can be brought alive by movement and sound effects, and programs which suggest things to do are valuable.

A toddler has a very short attention span, however. When she loses interest, turn the television off; if it is kept on as constant background entertainment, it will be hard for her to concentrate fully on other things, and play and books will have to compete with the television for her attention. Whenever you can, watch programs with a toddler, so you can talk about and help to explain them.

ENERGETIC PLAY

Babies gain control of their bodies very gradually, starting from the top and moving downwards, so they learn to hold their heads up before they sit, sit before they crawl and usually crawl before they walk. The rate at which different babies go through these stages varies widely and depends on personality as well as physical development. Like older people, babies differ in how active they are.

Once a baby is mobile, provided you take basic safety precautions (see page 25), it is better on the whole to encourage adventurousness than to overprotect. A liking for energetic play is good for increasing strength and agility, improving co-ordination and balance, developing self-confidence and sociability, and for all-round general health.

Finding enough space for energetic play can be a problem. Mother-and-toddler groups usually have more space than most homes as well as larger pieces of equipment such as climbing frames and ride-on toys. A park may have playground equipment basic enough for toddlers to try under supervision and at least gives them the opportunity to run until they are tired.

Even very young babies can be energetic and need the freedom to kick their legs and wave their arms without being restricted by too many clothes or bed-clothes. (See pages 8-9.)

Games to play

Physical play with another person is one of a baby's best means of communication; it also helps her to differentiate herself from other people, which she cannot do at first; it helps her to feel at ease with her body and is a good way of using up surplus energy before she is fully mobile.

Some babies enjoy these games more than others and physical play should never be forced on a baby who is not showing obvious signs of enjoyment. A baby is less likely to enjoy physical games when she is tired, unwell, hungry or overfull.

Tickling
Dancing
Bouncing on lap
"Flying"
Bouncing on feet
"Throwing" in the air
Piggy-back
Tipping up and down
Swinging

Exercises

Doing gentle exercises with a baby can be fun and increase his body awareness and control besides helping to develop muscles. Baby gym classes are held in some areas.

Arm stretch

Let the baby grasp your thumbs. Holding one arm down by his side, slowly raise the other above his head. Change arms.

Crossovers

With the baby either sitting up or lying on his back, open out his arms to his sides, then cross them back over his chest.

Bicycling

Hold the baby's ankles and gently rotate his legs, first in one direction, then the other. Also let him push his feet against your hands.

Wheelbarrow

With the baby's arms out in front of him, hold his hips and slowly raise his lower half. This is good preparation for somersaults later.

Encouraging physical skills

Don't forget that babies vary in how naturally physically active they are. While you can help a baby to practise the skills he is at the stage of acquiring and encourage him by praising his efforts, you cannot hurry him through the stages quicker than his body and brain will allow.

Holding head up

To hold his head up, a baby needs strength in his neck muscles. Put him on his front and see if he tries to raise his head and shoulders when you:

★ give him your thumbs to hold;

★ speak to him with your face just above his head;

★ shake a rattle just above his head.

Don't insist if the baby hates being put on his front.

Rolling

Being able to roll over gives a baby her first real taste of mobility and means she can at last get to toys that are just out of reach. To encourage her to roll from her back to her side, from about six weeks:

★ lie down alongside her, so she has to roll to get closer to you;

★ put a favorite toy out to her side;

★ kneel over her, then suddenly lower your face or a favorite soft toy. She may roll as she squirms to get out of the way. (Make sure she realizes this is only a game.)

Once she can roll, she may enjoy your nudging her with your head to make her roll or pulling her back with your hand whenever she starts to roll.

22

Sitting

Most babies cannot sit completely unsupported for about eight months but they appreciate sitting in a baby chair or being propped up with pillows or cushions* from about six weeks. A baby chair you can adjust from a reclining into a more and more upright position as the baby's back gets stronger is a good buy. If you prop the baby in her buggy in the corner or an armchair or on a bed** , ensure that there is a straight slope from her neck to the base of her spine. Putting the cushion under the buggy mattress helps. Propping the baby in a cardboard box can also be quite successful as the sides give good support.

To encourage a baby to learn to sit alone :

★ gently pull her up into a sitting position by her hands from about three months old. If she is ready for this, she will raise her head and try to pull herself up;

★ holding her under her arms, sit her on your lap or the edge of a table and speak to her. She may try to straighten up to look at you;

★ as her back gets stronger, say from about six months, sit her on the floor surrounded by pillows, cushions, duvets or rolled-up blankets,* perhaps with a folded blanket under her bottom and her back against an armchair;

★ sit her on the floor for a second and catch her as she overbalances;

★ give her toys that do not roll away and things she cannot easily play with lying down such as a spoon and saucepan lid to bang, an activity center and toys that fix to the high chair tray by a suction pad.

*Don't leave the baby alone like this. She could suffocate if she fell over.

Crawling

Some experts think that the co-ordination involved in crawling is good for the brain and develops the same parts that are used for later activities such as reading and writing. Some babies never crawl though, or else crawl sideways, crab-like, or shuffle along on their bottoms and this is nothing to worry about.

You do not need to put a baby in a crawling position. He will get there himself when he is ready, either from his front or from sitting.

★ Put a favorite toy a little way in front of the baby or, better still, sit holding it yourself.

★ Tempt him by opening a low cupboard that you would not mind him investigating.

★ Crawl with him. Have "races" and chasing games, and play hide-and-seek round the furniture.

★ Cut the ends out of a large cardboard box. He may like to crawl through it.

★ Give him toys that roll such as balls, plastic bottles and cardboard tubes.

★ Give him toys on wheels. Show him how these roll on their own down a slope. Gradually decrease the slope until it is flat and he may realize he can give the toy a push and then let go.

Once a baby is crawling, let him wear dungarees to protect his knees and don't confine him to a playpen.

**Don't leave the baby alone on a raised surface.

Standing

Many babies like to "feel their feet" from an early age.

★ Hold him so he can stand on your lap or any firm surface. At first his legs will buckle, later he will try to bounce.

★ Put him in a bouncer or walker (see page 24).

★ Put a favorite toy on a chair so he has to pull himself up to reach it. A baby learns to stand by pulling himself up on the furniture or people's legs. If you stand him up and then let go, he just collapses. Make sure your furniture can take his weight and that there are no cords or overhanging tablecloths to pull on.

When a baby first learns to stand, he cannot sit down again. Release his hands and lower his bottom gently to the floor.

Climbing

This usually starts with the baby trying to crawl upstairs and climb into armchairs.

★ Show her how to get down by sliding backwards on her tummy. Later you can show her how to come downstairs on her bottom, then how to walk up and down one step at a time, holding on to your hand or the wall.

★ Let her climb up and over you. This way you can save her when she falls.

★ Give her a giant floor cushion to climb on.

★ Give her an old tire.

★ Stuff an old cardboard box with newspaper.

★ Let her climb on and off ride-on toys.

Walking

Once a baby can stand, she soon starts inching her way along the furniture, holding on, then crosses small gaps (no wider than her arm span) between furniture, then larger gaps which entail letting go with both hands for a moment. Now she realizes she can stand alone and is almost ready to launch herself into space.

★ Arrange the furniture so she can make her way safely around the room.

★ Walk with her. She will let you know whether she needs to hold both hands, one hand or one finger. Don't let go to see if she can walk alone. It will shake her confidence and her trust in you.

★ Give her a baby walker: a large push-along toy on wheels. Make sure it will take her weight when she pulls herself up on it. (For another type of walker, see right.)

★ Stand a few paces away and encourage her to walk towards you.

Once she can walk on her own, you can give further encouragement.

★ She will probably enjoy carrying things about. Give her a bag to put things in.

★ Play fetching games (see page 17).

★ Play hide-and-seek around the furniture.

★ Play chasing games. These encourage running and are enjoyed most if there is a second adult to run to.

Toddlers find it quite hard to follow another person or even to walk alongside holding their hand. It is much easier for them to gravitate round a central point. Walking outdoors may be more enjoyable if you take the toddler to a park in a stroller and let her walk around while you sit down.

Bouncers and walkers

Many parents find these indispensable. Both satisfy babies' desire to be upright, besides strengthening their leg muscles and using up energy. A few babies do not like bouncers so it is worth trying out a friend's before you buy one. Walkers allow a baby to be mobile earlier than he would be otherwise but do not actually teach him how to walk as he does not have to balance himself.

Once a baby can get about under his own steam, interest in bouncers and walkers usually fades quickly. Don't leave a baby in either any longer than he is happy to be there, or for more than an hour in any case. Bouncers especially can be very tiring.

Pull-along toys

These become popular around the time the toddler realizes he can walk backwards and are good for improving balance and co-ordination. The best pull-alongs make a noise and have a low, wide base so they do not keep falling over. You can improvise some of your own.

★ Tie a piece of string to a rattle. Some of the home-made ones suggested on page 7 would work quite well. You could use a heated metal knitting needle to make holes in either end of a plastic container and loop the string through.

★ Thread cotton spools together.

★ Provide a cardboard box with string attached.

Indoor gym equipment

A plank of wood, about 150cm (5ft) by 30cm (1ft), with the corners rounded down, sandpapered and varnished is very versatile though, for safety's sake, you need to supervise its use closely.

For balancing, first flat on the floor, then raised on pillows, piles of magazines or a dishpan turned over. When you are helping a child to balance, try to give her your fingertip only; otherwise she will not learn to find her own balance but will use yours.

For sliding down and crawling up.

For jumping off.

For see-sawing.

Floor cushions, old mattresses and air beds are good for rolling and jumping on, and for breaking falls.

A stout hook in a ceiling joist can be used for a thick, soft rope about 4cm (1½in) in diameter, with a big knot in the end. Add a small platform and it becomes a swing. You may be able to incorporate the springy part of an outgrown baby bouncer so the toddler can still do some bouncing.

Balls and bean bags

Toddlers are too young for proper ball games and cannot usually catch but they like throwing, fetching balls for you to throw, kicking large balls and may enjoy toy bowling and passing a ball through a hoop.

For a change from balls, you could make a bean bag. Make a bag about 13cm² (5in²) out of strong cotton, fill it with beans and sew all the sides securely.

Safety

Once a baby becomes mobile, extra safety precautions are essential. Here are just a few things to keep in mind.

★ Keep all exterior doors and gates shut, and if necessary locked, so the baby cannot get out.
★ Make sure he cannot lock himself in the bathroom or freezer.
★ Use safety gates across the top and bottom of the stairs.
★ Put firescreens round fires and fix them to the walls.
★ Put safety plugs in empty sockets.
★ Keep harmful substances and dangerous objects high up where the baby cannot reach them even by climbing. These include bleach and other cleaning fluids, medicines, alcohol, perfumes, tools, razors, scissors, knives, pins and needles, matches, plastic bags.
★ Turn saucepan handles inwards so they do not stick out over the edges of the stove or use a stove guard.
★ Don't leave hot drinks or food where the baby can get them.
★ Use a harness in baby chairs, buggies and strollers.

MESSY PLAY

Play that can be described broadly as "messy" has a useful function to perform for babies and toddlers. It is important to avoid the idea that getting messy is naughty, as this restricts a child's range of experience so much. Instead, concentrate on ways of keeping the mess within limits. Careful preparation for this sort of play can help. If you cannot bear mess, it is best not to attempt the most messy activities, however much you feel you should. You both need to be relaxed for the play to be enjoyable. Children perceive mess differently from adults but the more cautious are often wary of new textures and sensations and dislike getting dirty themselves.

The activities on the following pages can play an important part in increasing the strength and control of the hand and arm muscles and in developing co-ordination between hand and eye. They also provide opportunities to learn about the feel and texture of different materials and to form early concepts of size, shape, color, quantity and capacity.

In a more general sense, they can stimulate the imagination and creativity, give a sense of achievement, and help to develop powers of observation, concentration and communication. Last but not least, many of these activities can be extremely soothing and relaxing.

Playing with paint

First painting sessions with toddlers are really just an opportunity to explore and play with paint. Children who enjoy mess will be happy to start "painting" very early. Those who are more wary of it may prefer to wait until they can hold and control a brush. It is probably worth having at least one experimental painting session by the time a child is two.

Protective covering.
If you have to worry about where the paint is going, it will take a lot of the fun out of painting sessions, so it is worth providing good protection for clothes and the painting area.

For overalls you can use an old shirt worn backwards with the sleeves cut down, a plastic raincoat cut to size, or a shopping bag with the bottom cut out and the handles as shoulder straps. You can buy plastic cuffs from good toyshops to protect sleeves.

For table and floor covering, use thick layers of newspaper, plastic tablecloths or cheap polythene sheeting.

Drawing

You can give a baby crayons to play with before she is able to use them but you will have to teach her not to put them in her mouth (if necessary by taking them away each time she does it). She will probably be able to make marks on paper with them from about 15 months onwards.

Before the age of two-and-a-half, children do not do much more than scribble on paper, first in straight lines, then gradually making deliberate curves and circles as well.

Try to draw things for your child. Even if you are bad at drawing, you can devise a few very simple pictures, perhaps by copying from her early picture books. She will enjoy seeing images she recognizes appear on the page. When she starts to talk, she will probably give titles to her own scribbles, however unrecognizable these may be to you.

Early scribble
Later scribble

Paint. Use fairly thick paint to start with. This is easier to control than runny paint and the texture is more interesting.

You can buy poster paints, specially thick poster paints called finger paints, or make your own paint by adding a little powder paint or food coloring to a thick paste. For the paste use wallpaper glue (non-fungicidal) or flour and water, or one of the recipes on the right:

---

1 Mix together:
  ½ cup soapflakes
  (not soap powder),
  ½ cup cold water starch,
  ¾ cup cold water.

---

2 Dissolve 1 cup cornflour
  in a little water.
  Add 1 liter (2 pints)
  boiling water.
  Boil until thick.
  Take off heat.
  Beat in 1 cup soapflakes
  (not soap powder).

If you mix a little dish washing liquid into the paint, it will wash off furniture and clothes more easily.

To begin with, provide just one color of paint. Later you can increase the color range gradually both for variety and the fun of mixing colors together.

Put the paint into any unbreakable container that will not be knocked over too easily. Margarine and large ice cream tubs are good.

Painting surfaces. You do not need to provide large sheets of clean white paper for early painting sessions. You can use a conveniently-situated washable surface such as a plastic-coated worktop, a draining board or even a window. Trays and plastic-coated chopping boards make good surfaces. Many toddlers are happy to paint on newspaper to start with. The back of left-over wallpaper, and wall and shelf lining paper are also useful.

Things to paint with. To get a toddler started, try spreading paint over the surface you are using with a brush or sponge and showing him how to draw in it with his finger, a brush or a stick. You can also provide other things to make marks in the paint with, such as kitchen utensils or a comb.

Brushes should be fairly short and thick for easy holding. A small decorators' brush works quite well. When you start providing more than one color of paint, try to have a brush for each color.

Show the toddler how to make prints with her hands and other things such as cut up vegetables, a paper cup or a washable toy.

Crayons. The best type to provide at first are short, fat, non-toxic wax ones. They are the easiest to hold, do not break easily and do not require too much pressure on the paper. Ordinary crayons can be a little sharp and dangerous if carried around. Don't let babies or toddlers play with lead pencils unless you can ensure they do not suck them.

Paper. Build up a supply of scrap paper, for example use envelopes unfolded, used wrapping paper and other packaging. It might be worth asking local offices if they have any scrap paper you could have.

You may need to stick the paper to the surface underneath to hold it steady.

Always bring out paper with crayons and put them away together if you want to avoid drawing on walls and furniture.

Playing with water

Where to play. The best place for indoor water play is the bath, where spills can be kept to a minimum. Start bath play early – pouring water for the baby to watch, making gentle splashes and, once he can sit up, giving him things to play with. The happier he is in water, the more likely he is to enjoy going swimming (see pages 36-37). Remember that bath play does not have to be restricted to "bathtime" but can be a good way of relaxing or cheering up a baby at any time of day.

Toddlers often enjoy standing on a chair by the sink, washbasin or at a bath table. You can buy plastic toddler basins which fit on the side of the bath. These can be ideal for water play.

Alternatively, put a dish pan or large plastic dish on the floor. Only put a small amount of water in it until the baby has learnt not to tip it straight out on to the floor. Put old towels or cloths down to absorb spills.

If you want to prevent clothes getting wet, you will have to take them off or provide boots and plastic raincoats or aprons. Plastic cuffs will help to keep sleeves dry.

In warm weather, bowls, buckets, hosepipes and sprinklers are great fun in a garden and an inflatable wading pool is a good investment.

Bubbles. Make bubbles by blowing down straws into water, squeezing empty detergent bottles or mixing one part dish washing liquid with two parts water and blowing through a bent wire or purchase a plastic bubble blower.

Things to play with. Besides proper bath toys, you can provide things from the kitchen such as plastic cups and jugs, spoons, a ladle, strainer, colander, funnel and an empty plastic bottle with holes made in it (use a heated metal knitting needle).

For a change, color the water with food coloring or paint.

Once a toddler enjoys imitating adults, suggest bathing dolls or washing up plastic cups and plates. Outdoors, provide a cloth and bucket for washing cars and tricycles, or a paint brush and bucket for "painting" walls.

Playing with sand

You do not need to have a sandbox in order to provide sand play. Just put a small amount of sand in an old dish pan or baby bath, or fill an old tire. Buy silver sand rather than builders' sand which stains clothes and skin.

Dry sand behaves rather like water so many of the containers used for water play are also suitable for sand. Toddlers may also enjoy sweeping it with a broom or dustpan and brush, weighing it on a set of balance scales or simply filling an assortment of containers with it.

Mixing sand and water together and molding the wet sand into shape is fun. Pastry cutters, jelly molds and foil or polystyrene food packaging all make good sand molds.

Safety and hygiene

★ Babies and toddlers can drown in very small amounts of water. Never leave them alone with it, even for a moment.
★ Cover hot faucets with towelling.
★ Clean sand by rinsing it with water containing baby bottle sterilizer. Cover sand kept outdoors.
★ If sand gets in someone's eyes, rinse them with cold water.

Playdough

Making playdough. You can buy playdough but it is a good deal cheaper to make it. The basic ingredients are flour and water. The recipe on the right makes a dough that has a pliable texture and will keep for several months in an airtight container in the fridge.

For variety, you could add food coloring or paint either to the water or at the kneading stage.

Mix to form a smooth paste. Put in a saucepan and cook slowly, until the dough comes away from the side of the pan and forms a ball. When it is cool enough, take the dough out of the pan and knead for three to four minutes. Soak the pan immediately.

Playing with playdough. It is worth seeing how a toddler reacts to playdough at about 18 months, perhaps earlier if you can stop her eating it. Show her how to squeeze and squash it into different shapes and make things for her.

Later you can give her some tools with which to make marks in it and cut it. Try plastic cutlery, popsical sticks and, when she no longer puts things in her mouth, bottle caps.

Playdough can be very useful when you are cooking. Give her some safe kitchen utensils and containers so she can imitate you.

Cooking

Playing with food and helping with cooking can provide children with a great variety of textures to experience and actions to perform. Small babies are often fascinated to watch cooking in progress; later they enjoy playing with kitchen utensils and vegetables.

At the stage when a toddler can control a spoon and wants to imitate the things he sees going on in the kitchen, you could try giving him a large bowl of pasta, oats or rice with a spoon and some smaller containers to put the food into.

Stirring and mixing are really the first useful things toddlers can do to help with cooking. Yoghurt dishes are a good idea. Just provide some raisins, chopped fruit, ground nuts, jam or honey to mix into it. Some people find instant mix cakes, crackers and desserts give toddlers satisfying results while being very simple to make. If you put a damp cloth under the mixing bowl, it will stop it slipping.

Cutting can be mastered surprisingly early if you start with soft foods like bananas, bread or large, flat mushrooms and use a blunt knife for safety. It is worth having an assortment of pastry cutters for cutting out biscuits and cookies.

Decorating dishes makes food seem more interesting to children and makes them feel they have had a big hand in the preparation.

Safety and hygiene

★ Get together all you need before you start cooking, so you do not need to leave your child unsupervised.
★ Teach children to wash their hands before cooking.
★ Teach them to be careful when handling knives.
★ Teach them to ask before tasting anything.
★ If you spill something, clear it up promptly. One of you might slip on it.
★ Don't let children touch electric appliances or the stove. Turn pan handles inwards or use a stove guard.

IMITATING AND PRETENDING

Babies can imitate other people during their first year, and learn some of their earliest skills this way, but it is not until they are into their second year that pretending really begins. To pretend, they must be able to remember things they have seen happen and to imagine that one thing is really another. Picking up a spare rag and helping someone clean the car is imitating. Taking a tea towel from the kitchen and wiping it over a toy truck is pretending.

Make-believe usually starts around the time a baby begins to talk. This type of play, and the talking aloud that often accompanies it, actually helps toddlers to learn to think and sort out ideas. It helps them begin to imagine how it feels to be other people and allows them to experiment with emotions of, say, an aggressive nature which in real life might be unacceptable or disturbing. In doing so, they can learn to come to terms with such emotions and to control them. In their fantasy play they are able to take charge of situations in which they would normally be powerless and this helps to build confidence. Make-believe can also be one of the more sociable types of play as children get older and so helps to develop social skills.

Make-believe is equally common and beneficial to both sexes and gives parents the opportunity to suggest reversals of the usual sex stereotypes, by giving boys dolls, for example, and encouraging girls to imitate do-it-yourself tasks.

The best role parents can play in imitating and pretending is to make casual demonstrations, such as building a tower of blocks or offering teddy a cracker; to join in make-believe if invited, for example to be a guest at a tea party or have a telephone conversation; to provide the few props that are needed for this age group and to try to allay any fears that may arise if fantasy and reality occasionally become confused.

Early imitation

Very young babies may try to mimic facial expressions. Full facial expressions of mood are not inborn but are learnt by imitation. Later, a baby learns to copy actions, such as clapping, and sounds, such as coughing and, very importantly, speech.

New skills are often learnt by imitation, but keep any demonstrations very casual and don't press the point. The baby may imitate you if you imitate her first. If she lifts her hand, try lifting yours, then waving.

Dolls, soft toys and puppets

These can be of great emotional value. They take on different roles as their owner wishes and so provide an outlet for all types of feelings. They also encourage talking.

In general, the simpler the toys, the more they stimulate the imagination. They need to be soft enough to be cuddly and the right size to fit the child's arms comfortably. A first doll needs to be a baby that can have things done for it. Dolls that can be bathed are often liked and ones that are flexible can be dressed.

First dolls' clothes should be easy to take off, if not put on. Try hats, socks, mittens, bibs, unbuttoned jackets, skirts with elasticated waists, ponchos or cloaks with self-fastening tape at the neck.

You can make a simple hand puppet out of an old sock or mitten. Sew on beads or buttons for eyes and a nose, and felt for a tongue, or embroider them in wool, perhaps adding woolly hair. For finger puppets see page 15 and for a wooden spoon puppet see page 6.

Around the house

By about a year old, babies are wanting to imitate the household tasks they see going on around them. Letting a toddler "help" will certainly slow you down but will give him a lot of pleasure, teach him new skills, develop his use of language and build his confidence. From a parent's point of view, there is something to be said for starting to teach toddlers how to be genuinely useful while they still see this as play rather than a chore. They often enjoy helping to:

unpack shopping
load and unload the
   washing machine
dust, polish and wipe
   up spills
sweep and wash
   floors
wash dishes (see
   page 28)
cook (see page 29)
make beds
tidy up toys
wash the car
dig the garden
decorate and
   do-it-yourself*

   The toddler will almost certainly prefer using small-sized real tools to toy versions. These work more efficiently in any case but make sure they are safe.

   Don't forget to provide encouragement by praising his accomplishments however small these may be.

   This type of imitating soon shades into pretending. Most early fantasy play revolves around the home and the roles played by the people in it because this age group has only a limited experience of the outside world.

   Useful props include:
Dolls, soft toys and
   puppets (see opposite)
The tools used for the
   household tasks
   mentioned above
The things listed on
   pages 10-11 under
   "Ideas for things to
   hold", especially –
   plastic cups, saucers,
   plates and cutlery
   metal teapot
   metal kettle
   saucepans

Dens

Toddlers often like having a den to hide and play in, usually in a corner of the room where you are. Drape an old sheet, blanket or curtain over a table, a framework of chairs or, outside, over a low clothes line.

Dressing up

This age group cannot really cope with dressing-up clothes though older toddlers may like a cloak made from interestingly-textured and brightly-colored material. You could cut down an old curtain (make sure it is not long enough to trip over), pull the gathering string up tight, cut off the loose ends, then sew on self-fastening tape. Dressing-up accessories can be enjoyed from an early age. Hats and bags are most popular but you could also provide:

Jewellery (Dip
   macaroni into
   water containing
   food coloring,
   let it dry, then
   thread on shirring
   elastic.)
Gloves
Shawls
Stoles (safer than
   long scarves)
Parasol
Apron
Purse
   A mirror helps toddlers to develop a sense of self and so progress to imagining themselves as someone else.

Cardboard boxes

These can play a versatile role in make-believe, representing anything from vehicles and buildings to furniture.

Paper plate
Dowelling
Cotton spools
Car
Red felt pen
Stove
Cheese box

31

With all these activities around the house, be very conscious of safety. See pages 12, 25, 28 and 29.

THINGS TO FIT TOGETHER AND TAKE APART

Sometime during the first half of the second year babies seem to enter a new phase of intense curiosity about the objects that surround them. They want to know what they can do, how they work and how their own actions affect them. They start experimenting with things to see what will happen, to solve puzzles and to achieve certain goals. They need activities and toys to satisfy and encourage this curiosity, which will help them to develop both physical skills and important new thinking skills.

The activities and toys described on the next few pages advance and refine the manipulative skills that have been developing since the baby's early months. They improve hand/eye co-ordination and strengthen the hand and arm muscles to allow for much finer hand control and delicate finger movements.

Handling objects and experimenting with what they can do helps children learn to identify similarities and differences between objects, to match like with like and to discover group identities. This is a very important step forward and leads, at about the age of two, to the ability to link information together to form mental concepts. The ability to think in this way is related to ability to use language and communicate.

During this period, toys you buy really come into their own. Exact fit can be hard to achieve in home-made toys but is an important element in these activities and produces the most satisfying results. Manufacturers are also better able to make toys light, smooth and unbreakable. Nevertheless, home-made toys can be useful for introducing new ideas, finding out what a child likes and providing variety.

When you introduce a new toy, you may need to demonstrate its possibilities by playing with it casually yourself. Don't try to show a child what to do with it, though. Freedom to experiment is the main point of these activities.

Fitting

Simple toys which encourage babies to place objects accurately, the right way round and the right way up, often become popular around the first birthday. Remember that round shapes are the easiest to deal with at first.

Lids. Provide a variety of containers, including pans, with lids to fit on and take off. Egg poachers are often particularly enjoyed.

Shape sorters and busy boxes. There are many different types of these varying in difficulty. A shoe box can make a good first shape sorter. First cut a round hole in the lid, just the right size for a small ball. When the baby can post this, cut a brick-shaped hole, then gradually add other shapes. Later she will be able to fit things like coins* and playing cards into slots.

You could introduce the idea of posting by demonstrating how to post a ping-pong ball down a kitchen or toilet roll tube.

Stacking

Cups. A set of graded plastic cups is an excellent stacking toy and can also be used for other purposes (see "Nesting toys" opposite).

Rings and balls. Plastic or wooden rings or balls stack on a central spindle, sometimes forming the shapes of people or animals.

*Take care until the baby stops putting things in her mouth.

Nesting toys. A set of graded plastic cups is the simplest and best nesting toy to start with and can be used for several other purposes too, for example emptying and filling, or stacking (see opposite). A set of plastic kitchen bowls might serve the same purpose. Paper cups and cup cake papers are fun for beginners but can be fitted together in any order and so are less challenging than sets of graded sizes. Plastic eggs and barrels, and traditional Russian dolls are more difficult to master but have a long play life.

First jigsaw puzzles. The simplest of these, sometimes called playtrays or inset boards, have pieces which have to be slotted into individual spaces. Some have knobs on each piece to make them easier to lift out. Others have pieces which can stand upright and be used for imaginative play. Some are helpful for learning about the things like colors and sizes. Others can be used later as templates for drawing round.

For variety, you could make a simple playtray. Cut some simple shapes out of a piece of thick cardboard, then stick the cardboard to another piece of cardboard the same size. Color in or paint the pieces to make them look more interesting.

Turning and screwing

The wrist movement adults use automatically for all sorts of practical tasks takes quite a bit of practice to master. Activity centers usually include a turning device; musical toys that wind up and toys with keys to turn also give good practice. You can also buy rods with variously-shaped nuts to screw on to them.

The difficulty in devising your own wrist-movement toys is finding things that are not too small and fussy. Plastic screw-topped jars and bottles*, nuts* and bolts, keys and locks are all good if you can find big enough ones. At a certain stage toddlers are often fascinated by doorknobs and faucets.

You can improvise some stacking rings that are not size-graded.

Piece of dowelling stuck to hardboard base.

Cheese boxes with holes cut in centre.

Cut-up kitchen or toilet paper tube.

Napkin rings

Used rolls of adhesive tape.

Bangles

Plastic bottle stuck to hardboard.

Blocks. A set of blocks usually has a long play life and is used for simple stacking long before being used to construct walls, buildings or layouts. You need quite a lot of blocks for building proper so, if you buy only a few to begin with, make sure you will be able to add to them later. Make sure, too, that different-sized blocks are in scale (whole, halves, quarters). Wooden blocks are more expensive than plastic but last longer and are more satisfying to play with.

For early stacking, you can use cans and packets of food as well as blocks.

Threading

You can buy sets of colorful blocks, beads and other shapes for threading. For beginners it is important that the hole in the center of each item is large and that the thread is fairly stiff or at least has a long stiff bit at the end.

You could try making your own threading toys from cut-up kitchen or toilet paper tubes, used small rolls of adhesive tape, curtain rings, or large nuts. For the thread use plastic or rubber tubing, or string attached at the end to a straw or piece of dowelling for stiffness.

You could also cut a simple shape out of cardboard, make some holes in it and tie on a threading device as shown on the right.

Hooks, snaps and zippers

Although this age group cannot master the skills required for dressing and undressing, they can start practising some of the techniques involved. You can buy plastic chains that pop or hook together and dolls with zippers, snaps and buttons.

Old bags and purses can give good practice with zippers. If you can sew, you could try making a cushion like the one shown below. Make the buttonholes large and don't sew the buttons on too tight.

Snap

Matching, grouping and grading

Many of the activities described on this and the previous two pages help children learn to match things according to their shape, size or color. Finding two identical objects is the simplest sort of grouping.

Can you find me one like this?

You can help to develop this ability further by encouraging a child to put assortments of objects into groups.

Can you put all the apples in the basket?

You can encourage an awareness of relative size by helping a child to grade objects in size order.

Which one is the biggest?

Is this one bigger than that one?

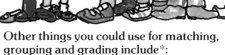

Other things you could use for matching, grouping and grading include*:

Vegetables	Crayons
Pasta	Tiddlywinks
Plastic cutlery	Buttons
Blocks	Stones
Small toy animals	Shells

Construction toys

These are toys which require a combination of the fitting, stacking and screwing skills described on the last two pages. The term covers a wide range of toys from simple pull-apart vehicles to complicated building systems. Only the simplest building systems are really suitable for children under two-and-a-half.

34

Take care with small objects if the child still puts things in his mouth.

WALKS AND TRIPS

Babies and toddlers need frequent trips out to avoid boredom, to broaden their experience, to meet people and, once they can walk, for exercise. Walks also provide opportunities for developing language if you talk about what you see.

Going out can also be more enjoyable for a parent than trying to entertain a bored baby at home even though, for longish outings, you have to plan ahead where you could feed and change the baby and have to remember to take all the necessary equipment such as food, drink, diapers, toys and comforter.

If a very young baby likes being in a sling, you can take him almost anywhere without much difficulty. Older babies and toddlers cannot keep still for long and need to get out of their buggy or car seat regularly for a break.

Local walks

These may seem mundane to you but everything the baby sees is new and interesting and, because his attention span is short, he appreciates the constantly-changing scene. If he gets bored, tie toys to the buggy or give him some shopping to hold.

Once a baby can walk, he needs time to investigate everything you pass. (See page 24 for possible problems with walking out-of-doors.)

Ideas for walks

The kind of outings you go on obviously depends on your individual circumstances. The local paper and library are good places to look for information about any special events in your area. Here are a few simple, general ideas for places to go:
somewhere to watch trains, boats or
  airplanes
a short train, bus or car ride (whatever form of transport is unusual for you)
the outside of a police or fire station
a building site or roadworks
a car wash
a duckpond
a farm park
a zoo
a pet shop
a library
swimming
  (see pages 36-37)

Long trips

Young babies are often lulled to sleep by the motion of travelling and it is sometimes worth planning journeys with older babies and toddlers to coincide with sleep times. You could also try these ideas:

★ Stick pictures on the backs of the front seats and the back doors.
★ Take along a varied selection of toys and introduce them a few at a time, perhaps loosely wrapped or in a bag for the baby to unpack. Tie toys to the baby's seat on short lengths of string.
★ Sing songs, recite nursery rhymes and play cassettes of these. Compile your own tapes of favorites.
★ Give small, frequent snacks of non-messy foods such as cheese, crackers, carrot, apple, seedless grapes and raisins.
★ Stop for about five minutes every hour for walkers to stretch their legs.

Socializing

Most babies love company and benefit from the attention and stimulation it gives them. They cannot understand the concepts of sharing or taking turns until they are about three and so cannot really play with other children until then, though they will happily play alongside so long as someone is there to keep the peace. Visiting friends with children and going to mother-and-toddler clubs provide invaluable opportunities for mixing with other children and starting to develop social skills.

GOING SWIMMING

There are several good reasons for taking babies and toddlers swimming. The most important is that they can get tremendous enjoyment from it; the younger they are, the less likely it is that they will be afraid of the water and strange places, and the more easily they will learn to swim; children with some experience of swimming are safer when playing in or near water; swimming is excellent all-round exercise and it can be a very sociable activity.

Opinions differ as to exactly what is the best age to start swimming sessions. Some people believe that after nine months in a fluid environment before birth, babies are born knowing how to swim and the sooner you introduce them to the water, the better. Spectacular results have been achieved with very small babies following specific methods.

However, many child care experts are unhappy about starting swimming too early because of the risk of cold and infection. Babies lose heat quickly and it is dangerous for them to get cold because their body heating mechanisms are less efficient than adults'. Some experts advise waiting until about six months, by which time babies' natural immunity is fairly well developed and they have had one, if not two, immunizations.

Developing confidence at home

The first step towards enjoying swimming is feeling confident in the water. A baby's first experience of water is bathtime so make this an unhurried, relaxing time for playing and splashing.

Bathing with a parent makes some babies feel more secure in the water and can be great fun for both.

When the baby can sit by himself, give him things to play with, including water wings.

Encourage him to float on his back or front while you support him. Move him backwards and forwards through the water, get him to splash with his arms and legs, and try to get him used to water on his head and face.

A toddler can get some idea of what to expect at the swimming pool by looking at books about swimming and by trying on a bathing suit and water wings.

First visit to a swimming pool

On your first visit to a swimming pool, it is a good idea to have a look round without actually swimming. This gives the child a chance to get used to the strange atmosphere, noise and smell without the additional strangeness of getting undressed and going in the water.

Swimming pool facilities

It may be worth travelling a little further than you need to find a pool with really good facilities for babies and toddlers.

★ What temperature is the water? It needs to be between 27°C (80°F) and 30°C (86°F) and for small babies should be at least 29°C (85°F). The air temperature should be one or two degrees above the water temperature.

★ Are there changing mats or tables for dressing and undressing babies, and playpens to put them in while you get changed?

★ Is there a separate pool for small children? It is very helpful to be away from the rough-and-tumble of the main pool.

★ How do you get into the pool? Some toddlers would rather walk into the water than be carried. Wide, shallow steps or a gentle slope are safest.

★ How deep is the shallow water? It is best if there is an area of very shallow water where a child can sit, crawl or splash about.

★ Are there classes for parents and children? These are an excellent idea especially if you yourself are not very confident in the water. If not, when is the pool quietest?

In the water

Your general aim is to get your child to feel confident and enjoy himself in the water. Keep each session short (10-20 minutes is long enough for this age group) but go to the pool frequently.

Hold your child close, with your head on a level with hers. Keeping eye contact, gently sink into the water up to your shoulders.

When he seems happy, hold him away from you, bounce him up and down, and move him backwards and forwards through the water.

Encourage leg kicking and arm movement.

Lay him on his back, supporting him under his hips with one hand, under his neck with the other.

Lay her on her front, supporting her under her chest with one hand, under her hips with the other.

Tow her along, holding her by her fingertips and encouraging her to kick her legs.

When she seems confident, let go for a few seconds. If she is reluctant, get her to pat a ball along.

When she is happy to move independently through the water, encourage her to change direction and turn from her front to her back.

Get her used to splashes on her face and head, then encourage her to put first her face, then her whole head, in the water.*

Water wings and toys

It is probably worth trying water wings from about six months. Buy the ones with double chambers and safety valves, and check for punctures before each session. Make sure they are small enough to stay on: they should be worn above the elbow. You can gradually reduce the amount of air in them until they are no longer needed. Many children refuse to wear them at first but, if allowed just to play with them, usually consent in the end. Nervous babies may appreciate a ring as well as water wings but don't use a ring alone as babies can slip through them. At the end of each session, have a few minutes without floating aids, so the baby gets used to the feel of managing without them.

Taking things like boats, beach balls, watering cans and bath toys to the pool helps to make babies feel more at home.

Hygiene and safety

★ Dress babies who are not potty-trained in close-fitting pants.
★ Watch out for slippery floors.
★ Teach toddlers to go to the toilet, blow their nose and go under the shower before getting in the water.
★ If you have to climb down a ladder into the pool, hand the baby to someone else while you do so. Teach toddlers to climb down backwards.
★ Always supervise young children closely even if they can swim quite well. Be especially careful with older children around.
★ Take a towel to the pool-side and wrap babies up as soon as they get out. Dress them warmly.
★ Don't take a child swimming if he has a cold or seems even slightly unwell.

37

Make this very brief. The reason children can drown so easily is that they do not know to hold their breath in water but automatically open their mouths to cry.

MUSIC, SONGS AND RHYMES

From the earliest weeks of life, babies find gentle music and singing soothing and relaxing. As they get older, they seem to like music with strong rhythms best. You can buy a variety of tapes, usually of nursery rhymes and songs, that are specially compiled to appeal to very young children.

Early exposure to many different types of music helps to develop babies' listening ability besides their capacity to enjoy music. Later, you can encourage them to follow their natural inclination to respond to music with movement and sounds of their own. Being sung to can also play an important part in both a baby's social and linguistic development.

Developing an awareness of sound

You can help a baby to learn to listen and become more aware of sound by drawing her attention to different everyday sounds and talking about them. Try pointing out the ticking of a clock, the rustle of leaves, rain falling, birds singing or an airplane going overhead. (See also "Things to listen to" on page 7.)

Moving to music

Older babies and toddlers respond spontaneously to music they like by swaying and dancing. You can encourage this and help them to let off steam by joining in.

Mirror dancing. Put some music on and dance together in front of a long mirror.

Mood dances. Do happy, sad, fierce or jolly dances. Toddlers usually find this amusing and it helps them begin to understand different emotions and feelings. You could also try alternating fast and slow dancing or dance like different characters such as a clown, a witch or a giant.

Bell dances. Buy some small bells from a pet shop and sew them on to elastic wrist, ankle, or head bands so the toddler jingles as she dances.

First instruments

Babies and toddlers enjoy joining in with music to make their own musical sounds. First instruments consist mainly of things to shake and things to bang.

Things to shake. Rattles are really a baby's first instruments. For suggestions for home-made rattles see page 7. Below are a few more ideas for "shakers".*

Jingle bells. Screw a ring hook into the end of a thick piece of dowelling and tie small bells to it.

Maracas. Put some pasta into two strong paper bags and fasten them to dowelling with string.

Tambourine. Fasten foil bottle tops round the edge of a paper plate with thread as shown below.

Things to bang. Try giving these to the baby from about six months. Saucepans, cake pans, plastic bowls and buckets, and coffee cans with plastic lids all make good drums when hit with a wooden or metal spoon. To make drumheads, tie wax paper over them.

Songs and rhymes with actions

Babies and toddlers love being sung to and some experts believe that this can play an important part in the "bonding" process between baby and parent. Sing or chant any songs that you enjoy yourself: nursery rhymes, lullabies, pop or folk songs, using tapes to help you if necessary.

Action rhymes and songs are a valuable form of entertainment for babies from about six months. The actions help to hold the baby's attention and, later, to convey the meaning of the words. Babies also enjoy the physical and social interaction involved and learn to anticipate the actions. The more energetic songs encourage body control and provide opportunities to use up surplus energy. The actions to the rhymes given below and on the next two pages are printed in the lighter type.**

This little pig went to market,
This little pig stayed at home;
This little pig had roast beef,
This little pig had none.
And this little pig cried,
"Wee-wee-wee,
I can't find my way home."

(Wiggle each of the baby's toes in turn, starting with the big one, and on the last line run fingers up baby's leg and tickle tummy.)

Round and round the garden,
Like a teddy bear;
One step, two step,
Tickly under there!

(Run finger round baby's palm. On the third line, jump finger up her arm and tickle armpit.)

Knock at the door,
(Tap forehead.)
Pull the bell,
(Tug lock of hair.)
Lift up the latch,
(Pinch tip of nose upwards.)
Walk in.
(Poke finger into mouth.)
Chin chopper, chin chopper,
(Tap under chin.)
Chin, chin, chin.
(Tickle under chin.)

Cobbler, cobbler, mend my shoe,
(Bang fists together.)
Get it done by half past two.
(Shake finger bossily.)
'Cos my toe is peeping through,
(Push right thumb through left fist and wiggle.)
Cobbler, cobbler, mend my shoe.
(Bang fists together.)

One, two, three, four, five,
(Count on fingers.)
Once I caught a fish alive.
(Wiggle hand to look like a fish.)
Six, seven, eight, nine, ten,
(Count on fingers.)
Then I let him go again.
(Pretend to throw fish back.)
Why did you let him go?
Because he bit my finger so.
(Shake hand as though in pain.)
Which finger did he bite?
This little finger on the right.
(Hold up little finger on right hand.)

Pat-a-cake, pat-a-cake, baker's man,
Bake me a cake as fast as you can.
Pat it and prick it and mark it with B,
And put it in the oven for baby and me.

(Clap hands in rhythm. On the third line, pretend to prick palm of baby's hand and draw a B on it. On the fourth line, pretend to put cake in oven.)

Incy Wincy Spider, climbing up the spout.
(Use fingers to show spider climbing upwards.)
Down came the rain and washed poor Incy out.
(Wriggle fingers, while lowering hands to show rain.)
Out came the sun and dried up all the rain.
(Raise hands above head and bring them out and down in a circle.)
So Incy Wincy Spider climbed up the spout again.
(Repeat climbing action.)

39

*Be careful with these until the baby stops putting things in her mouth.
**For more action rhymes see pages 71 and 72.

Clap, clap hands, one, two, three,
Put your hands upon your knees,
Lift them high to touch the sky,
Clap, clap hands and away they fly.

(Follow actions described.)

―――――――――――――

Baby's shoes,
Mummy's shoes,
Daddy's shoes,
Policeman's shoes,
Giant's shoes!

(Show length of each pair of shoes by
holding hands apart. Hands become
wider and wider apart.)

―――――――――――――

The elephant walks
Like this and that.
(Part knees and rock from
side to side.)
He's terribly tall
(Hold hands up high.)
And terribly fat.
(Hold hands out wide.)
He's got no fingers,
(Wriggle fingers.)
He's got no toes.
(Touch toes.)
But goodness, gracious,
What a nose!
(Wave arm in front of face
like a trunk.)

―――――――――――――

Row, row, row your boat,
Gently down the stream,
Merrily, merrily, merrily,
merrily,
Life is but a dream.

(Rock backwards and forwards
in rowing action.)

―――――――――――――

I'm a little teapot, short and stout,
Here's my handle,
(Put hand on hip.)
Here's my spout.
(Hold out other arm, bent at elbow and
wrist.)
When I get the steam up, hear me
shout,
"Tip me up and pour me out."
(Bend over to side of "spout", as
though being poured.)

I hear thunder, I hear thunder;
(Clap hands or stamp foot in rhythm.)
Hark, don't you? Hark, don't you?
(Cup hand to ear.)
Pitter-patter raindrops,
Pitter-patter raindrops,
(Wriggle fingers to show rain.)
I'm wet through.
(Feel clothes, then wring hands.)
So are you!
(Point to baby.)

―――――――――――――

Jack in the box is a funny wee man,
Sits in his box as still as he can . . .
Then up he pops!

(Crouch down and jump up on last
line.)

―――――――――――――

Eight big fingers standing up tall,
Two big ears to hear mummy call,
One little nose to blow and blow,
Ten little toes in a wiggly row,
Two fat thumbs that wiggle up and
down,
Two little feet to stand on the ground.
Hands to clap and eyes to see,
Oh, what fun to be just me.

(Indicate each part of the body
mentioned.)

―――――――――――――

Clap your hands, clap your hands,
Clap them just like me.

Touch your shoulders, touch your
shoulders,
Touch them just like me.

Tap your knees, tap your knees,
Tap them just like me.

Shake your head, shake your head,
Shake it just like me.

Clap your hands, clap your hands,
Then let them quiet be.

(Follow actions described.)

Teddy bear, teddy bear dance on
your toes.
Teddy bear, teddy bear touch your
nose.
Teddy bear, teddy bear stand on your
head.
Teddy bear, teddy bear go to bed.
Teddy bear, teddy bear wake up now.
Teddy bear, teddy bear make a bow.

(Follow actions described.)

_____

This is the way the lady rides,
Trit, trot, trit, trot, trit, trot.

This is the way the gentleman rides,
A-gallop, a-gallop, a-gallop,
a-gallop.

This is the way the farmer rides,
Hobbledy, hobbledy, hobbledy,
hobbledy,

And into the ditch!

(Jiggle baby up and down on knee in
different riding actions and on the last
line pretend to let her fall off.)

_____

To market, to market,
To buy a fat pig;
Home again, home again,
Jiggety jig.

To market, to market,
To buy a fat hog;
Home again, home again,
Joggety jog.

(Jiggle baby up and down on
knee in time to rhythm.)

_____

This little bird flaps its wings,
Flaps its wings, flaps its wings,
This little bird flaps its wings
And flies away in the morning!

(Interlock thumbs and flap
outstretched fingers, lifting hands
higher and higher.)

Here's a ball for baby,
Big and fat and round.
(Make ball shape with hands.)
Here is baby's hammer,
See how it can pound.
(Bang fists together.)
Here are baby's soldiers,
Standing in a row.
(Hold up fingers of both hands.)
Here is baby's music,
Clapping, clapping so.
(Clap hands in rhythm.)
Here is baby's trumpet,
Tootle-tootle-too.
(Blow through fists.)
Here's the way the baby
Plays at peek-a-boo.
(Cover face with hands, open them on
"boo".)
Here's a big umbrella,
To keep the baby dry.
(Draw dome shape over baby's head.)
Here is baby's cradle,
Rock-a-baby-bye.
(Make cradle with arms and rock.)

_____

Ring a ring o' roses,
A pocket full of posies,
A-tishoo, a-tishoo,
We all fall down.

The king has sent his daughter
To fetch a pail of water,
A-tishoo, a-tishoo,
We all fall down.

The robin on the steeple
Is singing to the people,
A-tishoo, a-tishoo,
We all fall down.

(Hold hands and skip round in a circle,
falling down on last line of each verse.)

41

GUIDE TO STAGES OF DEVELOPMENT

It can be useful to have some idea of the age at which babies and toddlers are likely to reach certain stages of development so that you can provide the encouragement and opportunity to practise new skills at the right time.

However, while babies and toddlers tend to go through the different stages of development in the same order, for example, learning to roll over before they learn to sit up, in reality there is a wide variation in the rate at which they go through the stages. For instance, learning to walk at any time between nine and 18 months is perfectly normal, although the average age is 13 months. For this reason, many of the developments described below and on the next few pages have been listed within fairly broad age bands. Where a lot of developments take place during a certain period, more specific ages have been given but these should be taken as a rough guide only.

The difference in the rate of development of different babies is accounted for not only by physical maturity, intellectual ability and the amount of stimulation received from the environment but also by personality. Rapid early development seems to bear very little relation to ability later in life.

It is also worth remembering that rapid progress in one area of development may temporarily slow down progress in another area. For example, learning to walk often slows down language development for a while.

Stage*	General physical development	Using eyes	Using hands
Birth	• Baby's position is all curled up. • When on front, can lift head just enough to turn it from one side to other. • When lifted up, head flops because neck muscles are not strong enough to support it.	• Only sees clearly things about 25cm (10in) from nose. • Everything looks rather two-dimensional. • Responds to bright colors. • Turns towards moderately bright sources of light. • Briefly follows object dangled about 25cm (10in) from nose.	• Hands are held in a fist. • Grasps objects placed in palm but this is only a reflex action.
6 weeks	• On front, can hold head up for a few seconds. • Can be propped up in sitting position with cushions or pillows.	• Watches faces intently when held in arms.	
3 months	• Body uncurled. Arms and legs free. • Lies on back with back of head on mattress. • Kicks vigorously. • Raises head when pulled into sitting position. • Rolls from back to side and from side to back. • Holds head steady when held upright.	• Follows adults' movements. • Follows object dangled 25cm (10in) from nose, both from side to side and up and down. • Watches movement of own hands.	• Hands held open. • Plays with hands. • Swats at hanging objects. • Can briefly hold objects placed in hands but does not yet look at them.

42

Remember that individual babies are unlikely to reach the stages at the precise ages given above. The ages are averages only.

The ages given for the toys and activities listed in the chart indicate when a baby or toddler is likely to start enjoying them for their main purpose. Some toys can be used in several different ways and so appeal to a wide range of ages. This is something to bear in mind, especially when buying toys. The more versatile the toy, the more it is likely to be played with and the better value it will be. Nesting cups are one of the best examples of this and have something to offer over almost the whole age range covered by this book. Young babies enjoy holding and examining them, then they can be played with in the bath, later they are used for nesting, a little later still for stacking and eventually are helpful for color matching.

If you introduce a toy to a baby and she does not appear interested in it, even after a casual demonstration, just put it away and try again a few weeks or months later. Although you can provide the encouragement and opportunity to learn through play, you cannot force progress or impose your own tastes. A baby has personal preferences just like older people and may never be particularly interested in certain types of toy, no matter what stage of development she has reached.

Listening and talking	Doing things for self	Suitable toys and activities
• Aware of surrounding noise, especially voices. • Startled by sudden loud noises. • Cries.	• Cries to make needs known.	• For the first few weeks of life, babies probably have enough to cope with just getting used to their new and totally strange environment. They need plenty of reassuring physical contact, gentle voices to listen to and faces to look at.
• Probably recognizes mother's voice. • Smiles at soothing voice. • Mimics talking by opening and closing mouth. • Gurgles.		• Things to look at (see pages 4-6). • Things to listen to (page 7). • Bouncing chair. • Massage (page 8). • Exercises (page 21). • Encourage to support own head (page 22).
• Turns towards sounds. • Can tell difference between one speech sound and another. • Chuckles.		• Things to swat at (see pages 8-9). • Things to kick (page 9). • Things to hold (pages 9-11), especially rattles. • Encourage rolling (page 22).

Stage*	General physical development	Using eyes	Using hands
4 months	• On front, lifts head and shoulders, taking weight on arms and hands. • Starts to roll from front to back. • If you support arms, can hold a sitting position.	• Can focus on objects at almost any distance.	• May try to take hold of things after measuring distance from hand by glancing backwards and forwards between the two.
6 months	• Raises head when lying on back. • Rolls from back to front. • May sit unsupported for a few seconds. • Bounces up and down when held upright with feet touching a firm surface.	• Watches toy dropped where can see it. If falls out of sight, forgets about it.	• Picks up either with both hands or one, using palmar grasp. • Transfers objects from one hand to other. • Puts everything in mouth. Grasps and plays with feet.
8 months	• May move around by rolling over and over. • Can sit unsupported if keeps still. • Gets into crawling position, and rocks backwards and forwards but cannot actually move along.	• Recognizes familiar faces.	• May offer things to people but cannot let go on purpose.
9 months	• Can reach for toys when sitting. • Can get into sitting position from lying down. • Crawls. May move backwards at first because arms are stronger and better co-ordinated than legs. • Pulls self up to standing position, using people or furniture. Can take weight on feet but cannot balance.	• Searches for toy dropped out of sight or hidden while watching.	• Starts to gain control over each finger separately and learns to poke and point. • Waves bye-bye. • Claps hands. • Uses pincer grip (finger and thumb). Can pick up very small objects this way and pull a toy on a string towards him by grasping string.
11 months	• Can sit down from standing position, using furniture. • Walks sideways, holding on to furniture. • Walks forwards if hands are held or when pushing baby walker.		• Learns to let go of things deliberately, then to throw and place them. • Uses objects to empty and fill containers.

44

Remember that individual babies are unlikely to reach the stages at the precise ages given above. The ages are averages only.

Listening and talking	Doing things for self	Suitable toys and activities
• Makes cooing noises: bah dah moo at first long vowel sounds, later adding first consonants. These early sounds are identical to all human babies. They are not trying to name anyone. • Blows raspberries.	• Puts hand to breast or bottle when feeding.	• Things to grasp (see pages 10-11). Bouncing on knee.
• Carries on "conversations" with an adult, making a sound, pausing for other person to reply, then answering. • Gradually stops making speech sounds that do not form part of the language she hears.		• Picture books. • Encourage sitting (page 22). • Activity center. • Bath toys. • Things to bang, e.g. drum, saucepan lid. • Baby bouncer (page 24). • Baby walker (page 24). • Swimming (pages 36-37).
ababab dada mama • Babbles in repetitive strings of syllables. • Shouts to attract attention. • Responds to own name. • Takes interest in adult conversation, even when not directly aimed at her.	• Holds, bites and chews crackers.	• Encourage crawling (see page 23). • Encourage understanding of words (page 15).
• Understands a few words, e.g. no, bye-bye. Bye-bye • Joins up a variety of different sounds into "sentences". Practises different intonation patterns.	• Grabs spoon when being fed.	• Encourage standing (see page 23). • Small things to pick up (page 12). • Songs and rhymes with actions (pages 39-41).
• Uses first words. Mummy Daddy Teddy These are nearly always labels for people or things and may be made up. • Uses voice to draw attention to objects or events, or to get help in doing something or getting something.		• Encourage walking (see page 24). • Baby walker (push-along type). • Nesting cups. • Letting go and dropping games (page 13). • Asking games (page 17). • Things to empty and fill (page 13).

Stage*	General physical development	Using eyes	Using hands
12-15 months	• Can lie down from sitting position without having to get on to all fours first. • Stands unsupported. Learns to walk a step between gaps in furniture, then to take first steps alone. • Crawls upstairs.	• Recognizes objects in books.	• Can hold two objects in one hand.
15-18 months	• Walks steadily for short distances. • Gets to feet without pulling self up on furniture and sits down without using furniture. • Climbs into adults' chairs. • Comes downstairs backwards on tummy. • Kneels. Bends down to pick things up without falling over when standing. • Carries things around in bags. • Throws balls. • Pulls and pushes large toys about. Pushes small wheeled toys when crawling.	• Imitates household chores. • Remembers where objects belong. • Recognizes landmarks when out.	• Can fit round and square shapes into holes. • Builds tower of three blocks. • Makes side-to-side marks on paper with crayon. • Turns pages of book, several at a time.
1½-2 years	• Runs • Walks backwards. • Pulls toys on string, first when walking backwards, then forwards. • Walks upstairs with helping hand, two feet to a step.	• Recognizes familiar faces in photographs. • Can match two identical objects.	• Uses wrist to turn knobs and screw lids. • Works zipper. • Starts using one hand in preference to other.
2-2½ years	• Can swerve to avoid obstacles and stop easily when running. • Walks up and down stairs, two feet to a step, with one hand on wall. • Squats on floor to play with toys. • Moves ride-on toy along, using feet against ground. • Kicks football. Throws small ball overarm. • Jumps in air or off a low step, both feet together.	• Begins to sort things into like and unlike. • Has increasing understanding of size.	• Builds tower of six blocks. • Does circular scribble with crayon. • Turns pages of book singly. • Can take candy wrapper off. • Hammers. • Can drum with two sticks.

*Remember that individual babies are unlikely to reach the stages at the precise ages given above. The ages are averages only.

Listening and talking	Doing things for self	Suitable toys and activities

• Understands several words when used in context.
• Understands simple instructions.
• Gradually increases vocabulary, learning new words at the rate of one to three a month.

• Helps self to toys if within reach.
• Picks up trainer cup and drinks without help but usually hands back to adult when finished.
• Chews well.
• Takes socks and mittens off.
• Holds arm out for sleeve and foot for shoe when being dressed.

• Encourage first words (see page 16).
• Fetching games (page 17).
• Hiding and finding games (page 17).
• Sand.
• Telephone.

• Brings food to mouth on spoon but cannot prevent spoon turning over.
• Takes off hat and shoes. Holds up arms when being undressed. Steps out of trousers.
• May indicate when diaper is dirty or wet.

• Copying games (see page 17).
• Dancing to music (page 38).
• Push-along toys.
• Balls to throw.
• Crayons and paper.
• Blocks and other stacking toys (pages 32-33).
• Shape sorters (page 32).
• Peg people, especially in vehicles.
  Equipment for imitating and make-believe (pages 30-31).

• Starts learning new words more rapidly.
• Points to parts of body when asked.
• Links two words together.

• Puts cup down after drinking.
• Takes arms out of coat.
• Helps to wash self.
• May ask for potty.

• Pull-along toys.
• Ride-on toys.
• Things to climb on, bounce on and slide down (see page 25).
• Story books.
• Jigsaws (lift-out and inset type (page 33).
• Playdough (page 29).
• Painting (pages 26-27).
• Turning and screwing toys (page 33).
• Threading toys (page 34).
• Musical instruments (page 38).

• Starts to form simple sentences.
• Vocabulary continues to grow.
• Different parts of speech, e.g. past tense, added.
• Grammar improves.
• Knows colors.

• Sits at table.
• Takes off trousers.
• Puts on mittens, hat, shoes.
• Washes and dries hands.
• Uses potty.

• Things to balance on and jump off (page 25).
• Football.
• Toy bowling pins.
• Things to match and sort (page 34).
• Hammer toys.
• Construction toys (page 34).
• Putting words together (pages 16-17).

SOME TOYS TO BUY

Below are just a few examples of types of bought toy that there has not been space to say much about elsewhere in this book. All the toys will not necessarily appeal to every child and they are not essential items of equipment but, in general, they are popular with this age group and have good play value.

Crib gym

These are useful to have across the crib when a baby is at the stage of lying on his back and is starting to reach out to grab things. They consist of a variety of objects to spin and rattle, grip and pull on. Besides helping the baby to realize the connection between his senses of sight, touch and sound, a crib gym helps to develop body awareness. He will feel the weight of his head and body as he tries to pull himself up by the grips and will strengthen his neck, arm and back muscles.

Rattles

As with other toys, the play value of rattles varies, depending on the eyes and mouth as well as hands and ears. Choose rattles that can be held in more than one way, that have moveable parts to encourage the baby to explore them with both hands and that have holes or grooves she can poke her fingers or tongue into.

Activity center

These have a long play life because the manipulative skills they require vary in difficulty, ranging from hitting and pressing to sliding and turning. Each hand action produces a diferent movement and sound, and so encourages understanding of cause and effect. Activity centers based on a theme (house, farm, fairground, for example) also stimulate the imagination and help to develop language skills as you talk about the pictures with the baby.

Ride-on toys

These are excellent for improving a child's co-ordination and balance, as she pushes the toy along with her feet against the ground and learns to steer. They are also fun to climb on and off and generally boost a child's confidence and sense of being in control. Always sit your child on the toy before you buy it to make sure it is the right size. Check, too, that it will not tip over easily and, important for indoor use in most homes, that it can be manoeuvred in a confined space.

Peg people and animals

These are good for developing use of the pincer grip, for shape matching if they can be slotted into vehicles or furniture, for sorting games and, later, for increasingly elaborate games of make-believe.

Steering wheel

The simplest of these attach either to the baby's car seat or buggy and often incorporate a horn. More complex ones, for slightly older children, have a dashboard complete with ignition key, gear stick and indicator levers. They are good for keeping a baby occupied when you cannot give him your full attention such as on car journeys, are an excellent prop for imitative and pretend play and, as the child gets older, may even help to develop rudimentary road sense.